I know that
you are **happy**
when you hop
and skip along.

I know that you are happy

when you giggle while you play.

I know that
you are **happy**
when you have
so much to say.

I know that you
are **happy**
when your games
are fun and loud.

I know that
you are happy
when you feel
grown-up and proud.

I know that you
are **happy**
when you try out

something new . . .

. . . and if you don't succeed at first,
I'll **help** until you do.

And when you are not happy

and the sky seems rather grey

I'll do my very best to chase

the gloomy clouds away.

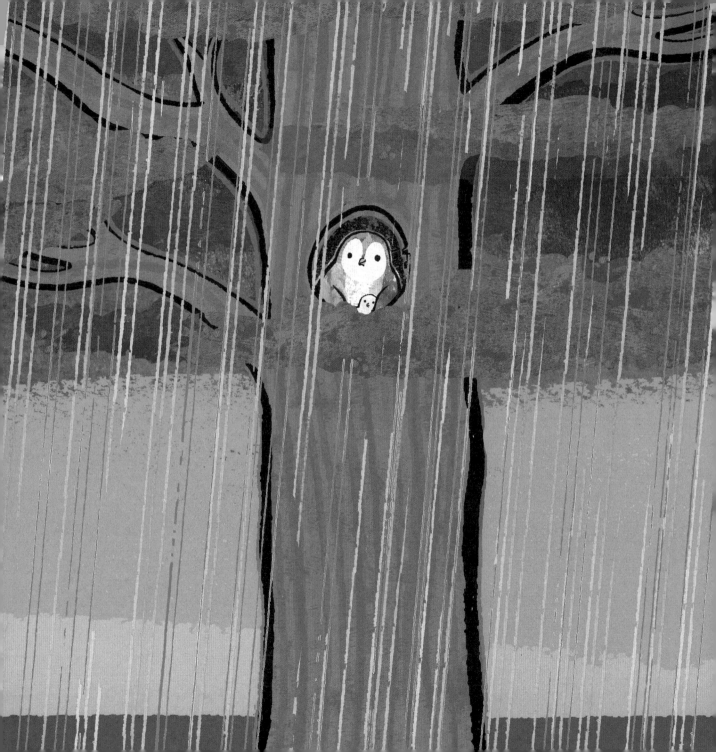

I love it when you cuddle close

and whisper, "I love you",

and I am happiest

of all . . .